James Alton James

English institutions and the American Indian

James Alton James

English institutions and the American Indian

ISBN/EAN: 9783337306007

Printed in Europe, USA, Canada, Australia, Japan

Cover: Foto ©Andreas Hilbeck / pixelio.de

More available books at **www.hansebooks.com**

Preface.

The Indian Department of our government, in nearly all its varied changes, finds a prototype, at times crude and again well developed, in one or more of the original colonies. There is to be found in the factory system, laws of trade, provisions for the acquisition of lands, annuities, presents, education, reservations, superintendents, and Indian agents of the United States government a very considerable of early colonial legislation.

The Indian has always been a subject for much discussion. The literature

on the "Indian Problem" has been unsurpassed by that relating to any other topic, except perhaps Slavery. Writers who have discussed this theme may be placed in two general groups: the one criticises any attempt to ameliorate the condition of the Indian through any governmental intervention; the other group sees only a series of wrongs from the first landing of the white-man, — the Indian dispossessed of his birth-right, maltreated and degraded.

It is not my purpose to be an historical critic

further than to note the growth of institutions [illegible] set forth in the various colonial records and colonial legislative enactments. I have not attempted a complete examination for every colony but have chosen Massachusetts, New York, and Virginia as types, noting any important changes or variations which may have occurred in the other colonies. While presenting the English I have referred at various times to the Spanish and the French policies. By such a comparison, human institutions become more

significant and high[illegible] [illegible]
[illegible] made notable.

I am indebted to Professor Herbert B. Adams, and to Professor Frederick J. Turner of the University of Wisconsin for many suggestions in the preparation of this book, and take this opportunity of returning my thanks to them.

James A. James.

June 17, 1913.

American State Papers I. II. III.

" " " IV. V. VI.

Adair, "American Indians".

Bancroft I.

Blackmar, "Spanish Colonization in the Southwest." J. H. U. Studies VIII.

Boyd Mss. Collection I – X. in Wisconsin Historical Library.

Bradford, "Plymouth Colony".

Butterfield, "Discovery of the Northwest".

Byrd Mss. II, III.

Charlevoix (Shea) II, III, VII.

Clark, "Indian Sign Language".

Dinwiddie Papers I, II.

Drake, "Biography and History of the Indians of North America".

Ellis, The Red Man and the White Man in North America.

Fiske, Discovery of America I, II.

Force Papers, I, II, III.

Franklin's Works I, II. Bigelow.

Gallatin, "Indian Languages".

Hale, [illegible]

Hazard, Annals Pennsylvania I.

[illegible], [illegible] II, [illegible] IV.

Hening, Statutes [illegible] II,

" " II, III, V, VII.

Hildreth, History of the United

States III [illegible]

Jefferson — Message to Congress

" "Inquiry"

Journal of Congress V, VI.

" [illegible]

[illegible]

[illegible]

[illegible]

" " [illegible] II, II. [illegible] VIII.

Records II, [illegible]

" Providence, [illegible]

[illegible] [illegible] [illegible]. V.
M[illegible] League of the Iroquois
M[illegible], history of [illegible]
Massachusetts.
M[illegible], "[illegible]" II, III
IV, VI.

New York documentary history, I–IV.
" col. documents, I, III,
" [illegible] II, I, IV, VI, VII.
New England hist. [illegible], XI. II.
North America — [illegible], 73.
New Britain [illegible]. I.

O'Callaghan, history of New
Netherland. III.

Parkman, Jesuits in North America.
" Pioneers of France [illegible]

Parkman, "Old France under
Louis XIV."

Perry, [illegible] II, III.

Pennsylvania Archives VI.

" Colonial Records VIII.

" Laws 1722.

" Historical Soc'y, [illegible] III,
vol. II, 2nd part.

[illegible] Colonial Records, II, V, VI.

" " " IX, X, XI.

Statutes of South Carolina II 1682-1716.

Stith, History of Virginia, I.

Schoolcraft, "Indians [illegible]
[illegible]."

" "[illegible]".

Turner, "Character and Influence
of the Indian Trade in Wisconsin"
J. H. U. Studies S. [illegible] XI

Washington, Messages to Congress.
" Maxims Inscribed.
Walker, Indian Question.
Weeden, "Economic and Social History of New England"
Winsor, "Narrative and Critical History of the United States" I, II, III, IV, V.
Wisconsin Historical Collections III.
Winthrop, History of New England I.

Contents.

7. Criticism on the Policy

II. Trading House System

III. Indian Slavery.

1. The Spanish Policy.

2. The English Policy.

in Massachusetts.

in Virginia.

in New York.

in Connecticut

Biographical

Introduction.

The Indians, when seen by the first Europeans, had made but little advance beyond the hunting and fishing stage. Tribal right to any particular region over which the tribe roamed; a territory wherein mounds or cairns were erected, can not be said to have been founded on any stronger basis than the right of present occupancy. Inheritance obtained in a few instances but conquest ordinarily accounted for

Hudson's Bay [illegible]
between the two great [illegible]
[illegible] the [illegible]
the [illegible] The earliest
territory of the European [illegible]
[illegible]
confined to the [illegible]
the state of [illegible]
[illegible]
[illegible]
[illegible]
[illegible]
[illegible]
[illegible]
[illegible] Brunswick, [illegible]

[illegible] west

from Cape Fear. The

and their [illegible]

[illegible]

the greatest [illegible]

[illegible], in general,

[illegible]

mountains [illegible]

[illegible]

classification into the tribes
noted have arisen from
the well marked distinctions
between Indian languages.

1. Minnesota Hist. Soc. Coll. V. 1. I

Iroquois Ascendency

The Iroquois, "the Indian of Indians, the thorough savage yet a finished and undeveloped savage", occupy a unique position in the history of the struggle for the mastery between the rival powers of France and England in the New World. During the seventeenth and eighteenth centuries the confederated "Five Nations" held the balance of power between these two contestants. No threats, promises, or acts of diplomacy on the part of the French ever fully broke the "chain" which bound the Iroquois to the English. Were it not for this deadly hostility

of the Iroquois to the French, New York might have been secured to Louis XIV. In that case the whole current of American history would be different and Federal Union be unknown." To this Indian League, France must chiefly ascribe the final overthrow of her magnificent scheme of colonization in America."[1] The Iroquois alliance with the English forms the chief fact in American history down to the year 1763. From it also arose indirectly many vexed questions which were settled on the part of the government

1. Morgan League of the Iroquois, 11

of the United States, only
after much diplomacy and
bloodshed. Why was their
fealty given to the English?
By what steps did they
become the "scourge of God"
upon the aborigines of the
continent?

At the time of the first
French and English
settlements they were rapidly
becoming the terror of the
whole country, outlying
isolated tribes were falling
rapidly under their conquering
might or were being scattered
in all directions. Says General
Walker: "It will not do to say
that, but for the Iroquois,

the settlement of the country by
the Whites would not have
taken place; yet assuredly,
that settlement would have
been longer delayed, and
have been finally accom-
plished with far greater
expense of blood and treasure,
had not the Six Nations,
not knowing what they
did, [illegible] began in
savage blindness and
fury, destroying or
driving out their other
tribes, which with them
might, for more than one
generation at least, have
stayed the western course
of American empire.

John Smith met some of their canoes at the mouth of the Susquehanna river in the year 1608. They were then on the way to attack their enemies.[1] The Delawares were defeated [illegible] water and coming out to put themselves under the protection of the Iroquois.[2] In the year 1651 they were [illegible] against

[illegible]
main[illegible]")

After the recoil of the Iroquois from the arquebuses of Champlain, they regarded the "gun as a deity," they saw, in this weapon, the superiority of their enemies and were willing to make any sacrifice to obtain it. Free traders from Holland traded a few guns to the Mohawks.[12] Four hundred warriors were soon

tries east of the Mississippi river. Before the year [illegible] they were victors over the Adirondacks of Canada. They had also taken possession of the territory situated between lakes Huron, Erie and Ontario and extending nearly to Montreal. "No distant solitude," says Morgan, "or rugged fastness was too obscure or difficult to escape their visitation; no enterprise was too perilous, no fatigue too great for their courage and endurance."(1)

Superior to the Tennessee river
and from the mountains to the
Mississippi. At various
places throughout their
territory, they founded colonies
in order that they might
maintain possession and
collect tribute. The power
of this confederacy then, as
a bulwark against the
advance of the French may
be easily comprehended.

It remains to trace the
Indian policies of the French
and the English as largely
developed through the
attempts of these nations to
gain supremacy over the
then powerful Iroquois

French Policy.

With reference to the general policy of the French, Governor Lewis Cass said: "There is a peculiar elasticity in French character. The Frenchman accommodates himself to any situation in which he may be placed. Upon the Seine and upon the St. Lawrence, if not equally pleased he is equally pleasant, and during two centuries, in the depths of the American forests, he has associated with their rude tenants, and as he could not elevate them to

always sought to hold the balance of power between adverse tribes. They desired to be the chief influence in Indian councils and tried to weave in the net-work of French power the most remote nations. French principles grew out of active relations with the tribes. Officers who administered the affairs saw the necessities of the situation and acted in accordance. The methods adopted were many of them similar to those by which Spain gained supremacy in the South. In turn, the English appropriated the means of

[1] Penn. Archives I. 5.

dictionary which had [illegible]
used by the French."

The advance of Cham[illegible]
in [illegible] war, [illegible]
[illegible]
[illegible]
[illegible]
[illegible]
[illegible]
~~Hurons~~ against their
Iroquois force.

Among the [illegible]
reach the first E[illegible]
[illegible] waste. [illegible]
[illegible]

[illegible]

[illegible]

[illegible] wilderness. They went [illegible] [1] [illegible]

[illegible] [2] [illegible]

[illegible] wilderness. When the French, [illegible] [3] [illegible]

1. N. Y. Col. Docs. II. 237.
2. N. Y. Col. Docs. I. 02[illegible]

in the council. They treated
the Indians [illegible] that [illegible]
[illegible]
[illegible]
[illegible]
[illegible]
[illegible]
[illegible]
[illegible]
[illegible]
[illegible](1) [illegible]
[illegible]
[illegible]
[illegible]
[illegible]

[illegible]

[illegible], [illegible]

[illegible]

[illegible] French [illegible]

[illegible]

[illegible] strategic [illegible].

[illegible]

[illegible]. Thus

was the most fruitful source of disagreement escaped. From a treaty of the year [illegible], the distinguishing points, calculated

to win the good will of the Indians, may be noticed. French families were to settle in the Huron country, suitable lots were granted on which cabins were to be erected. Hunting and fishing were to be in common. Indian protection was to be extended to the French. A generous supply of goods to meet the wants of the natives did not fail to win their good will or command their services.

The relations thus established between the French and the natives continued down till even after the extinction of the territorial

claims of France."(1)

The English Policy.

In the article previously referred to, Governor Cass says: "If any restraints were imposed by the British authorities before our Revolution upon the Indian traders, either in relation to their personal conduct, or the sale of their goods, such restraints have escaped our investigation. There was no attempt to provide a permanent residence for the Indians. There were no

1. Winsor, Narr. and Critical History II. 207

Indians and no efforts to introduce agriculture or the mechanic arts. There were no committees and no regulations to direct the conduct of the traders". The general policy of the English is weak at divers points. This criticism of [illegible], a reflection of the thought of his time, is without just foundation.

In their earliest dealings with the Indians, the original English settlement policy was quite different from that of the French. The English did not come for trade [illegible] through [illegible] to found an agricultural community.

these formed a background for the protection of the colonists as they passed out into the wilderness, establishing new settlements or carrying on their traffic with the natives.

Transfers of land.

In considering the English relations, it must be noted that the insecurity of position of the colonists rendered them [illegible] to transgress than [illegible] they were [illegible] one [illegible]. Its [illegible] [illegible] [illegible] that [illegible] the [illegible] [illegible], especially [illegible] the [illegible] [illegible]

[illegible] of the [illegible]
nation, later, the Indians
came to be regarded as
foreign nations, enemies of the
King, and article [illegible] of the
treaty of alliance usually
put the Islands [illegible] of
the tribe under the protection
of the crown![1]

When the [illegible] came to

of the tribes claimed all of the
land north [illegible] 2
north. [illegible]
[illegible], [illegible] tracts [illegible]
by [illegible]. Then [illegible]
have [illegible]
[illegible], [illegible]
[illegible]
his land. Price has [illegible] drawn
to him until the whites made
purchases. Mr. Harlan states:
that the [illegible] of land from
the natives [illegible] to the
white settlers has been [illegible]
in [illegible]. Mr [illegible]"
[illegible] says; "That the [illegible]
[illegible] soil is in the [illegible]
[illegible] intelligence, [illegible]
[illegible]

resolute and enduring integrity.[11] It is to be remembered that the New England Indians were soon reduced by the Europeans and did not at first impede the succession of the Puritans.

Purchase of land from the Indians, without license from the General Court, was prohibited by the early legislature of Massachusetts. The natives were to have the right to [illegible] [illegible]. Governor Winslow of Plymouth in his report to the Federal Commissioners in 1676 confirms the statement that there was an attempt at justice on the

Weeden, Economic History of New England [illegible]

part of the colonists in their
early relations with the Indians
regarding the land purchases.
What we say of Plymouth
seems to have been equally
true of the other colonies.
He says: "I think I can clearly
say that before these present
troubles broke out, the
English did not possess one
foot of land in this colony
but what was fairly obtained
by honest purchase of the
Indian proprietors. Nay
because some of our people
are of a covetous disposition,
and the Indians are in their
straits easily prevailed with
to part with their lands we

first made a law that none
should purchase or receive
of gift any land of the Indians
without the knowledge and
allowance of our Court.
And if at any time they have
brought complaints before us,
they have had justice
impartial and speedy, so that
our own people have fre-
quently complained that we
erred on the other hand in
showing them overmuch favor.

The last Hampton Book
of Laws for the New York
Colony provided that no
purchase of lands from
the Indians after the year
1664 should be valid . .

the archives of the time were brought by the purchaser before the governor. After satisfaction was rendered the Indians, the lands were recorded in the colonial office.[1] One of the transfers of 1683 may be noted as typical. The conveyance consisted of lands owned by the Cayugas and Onondagas, situated on the Susquehanna river and included their right to the river itself. They were to receive in return, "a half piece of Duffels, Two Blankets, Two Guns, Three Kettles, Four Coats, Fifty lbs. of Lead, and five and twenty

1. N. Y. Hist. Soc. Coll., 1869, 354

lbs. of powder".

Governor Burnet in 1721 sent the following order to his agent; "When you have pitch'd upon a convenient place for a Trading house you are to endeavor to purchase a Tract of Land in the Kings Name and to agree with the Sinnekees for it which shall be paid by the Publick".[2]

The policy instituted by Penn[3] seems to have been followed by the colony of Pennsylvania throughout its subsequent history. All differences were to be settled by a tribunal

both parties should be represented[11]. No lands were to be sold any private persons by the Indians, nor was any purchase valid except that made by Penn or his Commissioners[12]. Any who refused to submit to such ruling, not only lost the land he bought but was subject to a fine of ten shillings for every one hundred acres so purchased[13].

As has been noted, the Delawares were subdued before Penn's coming and would doubtless have graciously submitted to a code less just. Such

the strictness of the rulings in behalf of justice towards this almost vanquished tribe, that hunters on Indian lands not purchased by the proprietor, were fined fifty pounds or were imprisoned twelve months. For every offense against the law, regarding the survey of unpurchased lands, there was a penalty of five hundred pounds and twelve months imprisonment without bail.

Land, forming the present site of Philadelphia, was purchased by Thomas Holme, President of the Council during the absence of Penn in [illegible]

The "treaty" was agreed to by the Indians in consideration of [illegible] fathoms of wampum, 20 [illegible], 20 [illegible], 20 [illegible] of stroud waters, 20 kettles, 20 shirts, 20 [illegible], 2 [illegible], 20 [illegible], 20 pair scissors, 20 combs, 20 [illegible], 20 knives, 20 [illegible], 20 bars of lead, 20 pounds of powder, 20 [illegible], 20 looking glasses, 20 [illegible], 3 papers of [illegible], 20 [illegible], 20 [illegible] of [illegible], [illegible], [illegible]."[1]

It was [illegible] by the [illegible] of [illegible] [illegible] the circumstances:

1. Memoirs of Hist. Soc. of Penn. Vol. II part 2.

"The purpose to proclaim and make it known to them all, [illegible] [illegible] [illegible] [illegible] [illegible] that our community [illegible] is to [illegible] in their country, yet not to supplant and [illegible] them out but to bring them from their [illegible] condition to a [illegible] better"[1] [illegible] in the year 17[illegible] [illegible] that he [illegible] [illegible] [illegible] [illegible] that [illegible] [illegible] [illegible] by the Indians, they are [illegible] such a change [illegible] [illegible] [illegible] [illegible] [illegible] [illegible] mankind.[2]

We find no general superintendence of the Indians anterior to 1755. Other than that exercised by the courts of the colonies with the several governments of the colonies, Commissioners were appointed from time to time.

The General Court of Massachusetts allowed certain Indian villages to choose their own magistrates. These were to be approved by the Superior Court. One of these magistrates, together with an English magistrate constituted a higher court having jurisdiction commensurate with that of the county court. Their control was limited to [illegible] criminal cases, the lands set apart for the Indians and to the maintenance of

founding of schools.

New York was the central colony. The influence of a policy adopted at Albany was tacitly accepted by her sister commonwealths. Sir William Johnson was appointed superintendent of Indian affairs.[1] He was well received from the first by the Indians. He found the department which had been thoroughly disorganized under the rule of Commissioners. His services during the first part [illegible] did the commissioners again take control. General dissatisfaction was expressed until 1755 when Superintendent Johnson was permanently

(1) N. Y. Col. Docs. VII.

adopted. This result was brought about through the meeting at Albany in 1754 of commissioners from six provinces.[1] From their proceedings we learn that each tribe was to have a resident agent who was to have no concern in the trade, who was to communicate with the superintendent regarding his particular district. The superintendent was, in turn, subject to advice from the Crown. Trade with the Indians was to be

Indian War was to cause a re-organization of the relations for diplomatic intercourse [illegible] with the Indians on a wider basis. [illegible] was [illegible] the [illegible] the [illegible], [illegible] treaties between the [illegible] and the [illegible], [illegible] that the [illegible] were [illegible]; [illegible] of the [illegible]; [illegible] upon [illegible] that [illegible] demand.

Their [illegible] [illegible]

[illegible] [illegible] hinder [illegible]

my english in [illegible]

english & Dutch

Africa to-day [illegible] the

[illegible] [illegible] of the

They explain the

[illegible] yet the [illegible]

are able to [illegible]

[illegible] higher [illegible]

That there was

trade among the [illegible]

to the coming of [illegible]

American [illegible] to [illegible]
The earliest [illegible] sick
[illegible]
[illegible] by the [illegible]
[illegible]
[illegible] from [illegible]
[illegible] in [illegible]
[illegible]tions, [illegible]
[illegible]
[illegible]ned [illegible]
in language [illegible]
[illegible] signs.[1]

[illegible]
[illegible] had [illegible], [illegible]
[illegible]
[illegible] they [illegible]
practiced in [illegible]
[illegible]. The Indian [illegible]
[illegible]

colonist but ended [illegible]
[illegible];
but in the great [illegible] of the
[illegible],
[illegible]
nation.

On the [illegible]
[illegible]
[illegible],
[illegible]
[illegible]
[illegible]
[illegible] struggle
against famine and disease.
How the settlers [illegible]
[illegible]
[illegible]
[illegible]
[illegible],

among them with presents.

By the end of the [illegible] century,
the whites [illegible]
great [illegible], and [illegible]
[illegible] that the [illegible]
[illegible] of arms among some
of the tribes. The Narragansetts
could raise five hundred men
[illegible] the [illegible] at one
time!

Even before their acquisition
were supplied [illegible]
began to traffic [illegible].
[illegible] in small quantities
was introduced into New England
by Dutch traders, in exchange
the Indians brought their beaver

beaver-skins were brought to the Dutch from the Great Lake during a single year.

"The settlement of the first year, the [illegible] with [illegible] sent out a shallop — [illegible] the [illegible], [illegible] [illegible] [illegible] [illegible] with [illegible] [illegible] and [illegible]."[1] The [illegible] the colony and [illegible] the trade, [illegible] [illegible] their [illegible]

other forms to [illegible]

From this same [illegible] [illegible] see that the [illegible] [illegible] under the [illegible] [illegible] [illegible] [illegible] [illegible]

The economy [illegible] increased [illegible] [illegible] [illegible] that this [illegible] [illegible]

each single Decima
buy a share and [illegible]
of a family might have
so many shares in
[illegible] in his family
company was [illegible]
its accounts, he had
let in 1627 to a company
of undertakers, for
period of six years,
this time it was to [illegible]
[illegible] to the [illegible]
At the [illegible]

followed every man th

[illegible] the colonists [illegible]

was to put in his "proportion" under his own name or Amos may put in under the name of some one whom they generally trust and are satisfied in". The matter here to be called undertakers [illegible] [illegible] the undertakers. In each [illegible] the undertakers were to choose "committees" of two or three to manage the joint stock. This management was to consist in "buying commodities for the trade, setting trading [illegible], hiring [illegible] [illegible] [illegible] the [illegible], receiving the [illegible] [illegible] the [illegible] [illegible] [illegible] [illegible] [illegible] [illegible] [illegible] to [illegible] [illegible]

may be necessary and [illegible]". This way of trading was to continue for ten years. The [illegible] [illegible] [illegible] [illegible] [illegible] [illegible] [illegible] [illegible] [illegible] [illegible] [illegible] [illegible] the payment of [illegible] [illegible] [illegible] the managers [illegible] [illegible] [illegible] [illegible] by the undertakers, the profits were to be divided. Each [illegible] was to [illegible] [illegible] such [illegible] [illegible] as the commissioners in conjunction with the committee [illegible] [illegible].

Previous to the ratification of the aforementioned [illegible], [illegible] [illegible] [illegible] [illegible], [illegible], [illegible] [illegible] the [illegible] trade for three years to a trading company.[1] The [illegible] [illegible]

1. Mass. Records III 53. 54.

of the company were probably purchased by the United Colonies. At any rate, there was a [illegible] trade for the United States. The stock seems to have been much smaller than that originally recommended.

Massachusetts was an old encroaching partner in the Union. While the [illegible] of trade did not [illegible] the [illegible] of the [illegible], the [illegible] [illegible] [illegible] [illegible] to the [illegible] [illegible] [illegible] Massachusetts Bay and Plymouth [illegible]. Finally in 1657, Massachusetts Bay Colony declared that the trade [illegible] [illegible] [illegible] jurisdiction should [illegible]

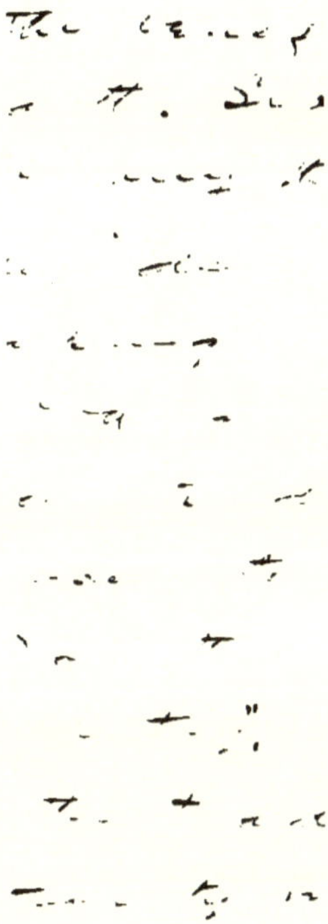

of advantages and ways accruing to the country by virtue of the increase of prince, namely, commerce, with cattle, furs in return, from which to be traded with the Indians, together with the rates of having of prince from the [illegible] [illegible]," it the [illegible] of this form the trade [illegible] [illegible] into the [illegible] of the colony.

Trade was at first [illegible] carried on [illegible] [illegible] by private traders, [illegible] to restrain these traffickers from taking undue advantage of the natives [illegible] [illegible] the [illegible] [illegible]

new requirements [illegible] to [illegible] [illegible] [illegible] [illegible].[11]

The Virginia assembly of 1637 [illegible] [illegible] [illegible] [illegible] [illegible] [illegible] chance. This act was repealed two years later and trading with the Indians was punished by imprisonment at the discretion of the governor and council.[14] In 1656 all freemen were given the privilege to trade without [illegible] restriction. Virginia again found it necessary to limit this freedom by bringing the Indian trade more completely under governmental surveillance.

This led to the [illegible] trial in [illegible], establishing [illegible]

throughout the colony. There were to be seven, they were held at places designated by the justices of the peace in the different counties, on the James, Rappahannock, and Potomac rivers and Accoma- and Northampton counties respectively. The meeting at these stated places occurred twice each year and the affairs continued "forty days and no longer".

The Indians were to be allowed to bring any commodities which they might wish to trade, and sell or truck, for the same with the English resorting thither, but not elsewhere nor for any

commodities whatsoever, by
Englishman who traded with
the Indians at any other times
or places was to be fined
2000 lbs. of tobacco for each
offense, one-half of which
was to go to the informant and
the remainder to the colony.

Provision was made for
the appointment by the governor
of a clerk, in case the county
clerk did not serve, at each
of these fairs, whose duties were
to keep account of all articles
bought and sold, in payment
of the clerk's fee [illegible]
was set aside, the governor's
[illegible].
Although fairs seemed a good

method for the execution of the provisions of trade, they were abandoned. Virginia, in 1691, repealed all acts which limited and restrained free trade with the Indians."

So long as the Indian was unsupplied with fire-arms the various regulations enacted to insure a generally peaceful trade. When he first learned the use of the gun he was no longer willing to submit to the bargaining dealing by the white man but set up for himself. From the time when the Dutch furnished the first arms among the Iroquois

Indians were willing to make any sacrifice to obtain the coveted treasure, [illegible] private traders were [illegible] to supply them. [illegible] the trade would seem to the Indians [illegible]. Then came [illegible].

[illegible] the [illegible] trade, [illegible] 33 [illegible] that [illegible] the [illegible].

wonder, "he lustily exchanges
for a couple of deer"[1] This
colony when it entered on
a monopoly of the Indian
trade in 1657, passed an act
that no person should trade
with the Indians except [illegible]
[illegible] granted a license.
There was [illegible] the [illegible]
There was also [illegible] the
[illegible], however,
that [illegible],
this [illegible]
[illegible]
During the course of a
century before the overthrow
of French power, the English
[illegible] in [illegible]
they [illegible] to [illegible]

1. N. Y. Col. Doc's. I 243.

[illegible],

Franklin saw clearly the need for much regulation on the part of the English. In the plan of Union for 1754 he urged upon the Commissioners from the colonies: "That they make such laws as they judge necessary for regulating all Indian trade. He adds: Many quarrels and wars have arisen between the colonies and Indian nations through the bad conduct of traders who cheat the Indians after making them drunk, & the

great expense of the colonies both in blood and treasure, particular colonies are so interested in the trade as not to be willing to admit such a regulation as might be best for the whole; and therefore it was thought best under a general direction."(1)

After the outbreak of hostilities between England and France, the English exercised still greater care in the protection of the Indian trade. A proposed plan of Secretary Pownall set forth an almost ideal Indian agency. Its features were about as follows: It advocates an intendant of

(1) N. Y. Col. Docs. VI 27

trade to reside at issues. His inducement is to receive a stated salary and is not to be in any way concerned in the Indian trade. His duties are to endeavor to discover all frauds and impositions on the Indians; to inspect all weights and measures and see that they are of an equal standard. He is to bring all offenders to trial before the commission officer of the garrison and send all convicted to New York in irons. In addition, no trader is to presume to carry on trade unless he has a license from the commandant.

Every trader is to give bond of 500 $'s, that he will observe all game regulations. The government is to have the privilege of [illegible] any instructions to any [illegible], to [illegible] the Intendant.

The English attitude [illegible] in regard to the trade after the war of 1763, [illegible] begun in 1764 [illegible] by the [illegible] instructions [illegible] [illegible] to the [illegible] of the [illegible] that [illegible]

[illegible] from the governor, that were they then to be limited to [illegible] beyond the [illegible] in direction settlements.[1]

It is worthy of note that the chief cause for the calling together of the commissioners from the several colonies in 1754, was the desire to make some general plan for the Indian trade, or the necessity of trade regulations needed to maintain relations with the savages. May it not be said that in these trade negotiations was established that common feeling of trust [illegible] that was to end in the final Union [illegible]

1. Colden Letters [illegible] N. Y. Hist. Soc. Coll. [illegible]

attainings.

In [illegible] the assemblies of the colonies were given the power to regulate the Indian trade. As this was not effective, [illegible] in the [illegible] [illegible] [illegible] [illegible] [illegible] in [illegible] [illegible] [illegible] nations [illegible] [illegible] [illegible] colonies. Patrick Henry was the commissioner from Virginia. But as there was not a complete representation from all the

colonies, no definite plans
for trade with the Indians
seems to have been formulated.

James Russell Lowell says: "The
temperance question agitated
the fathers very much as it
still does the children. We
have never seen the anti-
prohibition argument more
cogently stated than in a
letter of Thos. Shepard, minister
of Cambridge to Winthrop, in
1639: 'This also I cannot humbly
intreat, that there may be no
law made of drinking in
any case one to another, for
I am confident as that
stands here will fall much
be kept from his counsels

by the same arguments; we
aver that the commandment
was in every case, and the
thing [illegible] to lead a man
to make more than temples
yet [illegible] himself
hath made".[11]

Whatever [illegible] might
have been [illegible] among
themselves, the [illegible] early
learned to fear the [illegible] —
figures in the [illegible].
Because [illegible]
the [illegible] state to [illegible]
their [illegible] against [illegible]
in [illegible]. It meant [illegible]
[illegible] that [illegible]

at the plantations because of the traffic in rum. Rum had the effect making them Massachusetts Bay and Plymouth Colony set a fine or imposed commonly with the punishment for [illegible] [illegible] sold". Traders were guilty of same, paid their fines and continued their traffic. The Indian did not cease to have the desire for "fire-water" because of a fine of ten shillings or a shilling for drunkenness.

it with that of the French.
Under the English the results
induced the Iroquois of the
[illegible], discouraged [illegible]
[illegible], [illegible] [illegible], to [illegible]
in the [illegible], they were [illegible]
[illegible] to make use of [illegible]
[illegible] Jesuits, French or
English [illegible] [illegible] [illegible]
the [illegible] of [illegible] [illegible] [illegible]
[illegible], [illegible] [illegible] of [illegible]
whatever became of their
employers". He set forth the
manifest superiority of the
French system and made
suggestions for the future
improvement of the [illegible]
methods.

Trading [illegible] System

This method of trading with the Indians was in use [illegible] [illegible]

[illegible]

[illegible][1]

[illegible]

1. Mass. Hist. Coll. 5 s. III 233

peace, 'commerce &c", were started in two trading houses in order to meet the trade which had previously been carried on with the Indians by fishermen. By an act of 1632, the Court of Boston ordained 'that there shall be a trucking house appointed in every plantation, whether the Indians may resorte to trade, to avoide there comeing to severall houses".

But the terms were not used with their full intent until the year 1694. Massachusetts Bay colony in that year, through her governor, council, and representatives passed an act

for regulating the Indian trade[1]
This enactment contains a
complete description of the
trading house system, as
it forms the basis for the
establishment of all future
trading houses, I shall
consider its provisions some-
what at length. All trade with
the eastern Indians was to be
carried on "at the charge of
and with the publick stock in
their majesties' treasury
within this province and for
the benefit and advantage of
the same". Truck-masters
were provided for. They were
to be appointed by the treasurer
and the commissioner of impost,

1. Province Laws Mass. Bay Colony 1692
I sec.

These managers of the trade were to have a stated salary and to take an oath that they would not engage in trade on their own behalf. Instructions regarding the trade were to proceed from the governor and council. From time to time the accounts were to be laid before the General Court. It was further provided: "That no person or persons whatsoever, other than those to be employed as spoken of, shall directly or indirectly truck, buy, sell, deal or trade with any Indian or Indians under penalty of 50 £'s and forfeiture of goods."

The original stock was
stocks. Any gains in the trade
were used for the support
of the government". Upon the
renewal of the act in 1711,
it was provided that the
original investment with gains
was to be reinvested in the
trade. The reason for this
increase of capital stock is
that the "French shall by all
means be undersold". This
was continued the policy and
for the early establishment of
trading houses.

French influence compelled
a more extended trade by
the colony. The friendship of
the Indians was by all means

to be maintained. In the year 1725, 400 £'s were given for the support of trade at the different truck-houses.[1] The plan is here to buy the goods at wholesale prices and to sell their fur at the Boston market rates,[2] and agent who violated either of these regulations was upon conviction to be fined 100 £'s.

Acts providing for Trading houses were continued and renewed by the colony at various times until and during the Revolutionary War. The year 1753 is of special note in the history of this system. It marks the passing

1. Province Laws Mass. B. Colony 1725 II sec. 1.
2. Province Laws Mass. B. Colony 1725 II sec. 4.
See acts 1731, 1733, 1737, 1742, 1753, 1760, 1762

of the men from Massachusetts to Pennsylvania. This, as is characteristic, was but one more strand in the ultimate acceptance of the method of the general government. Franklin was appointed agent of the Indians on the Ohio river. In the year 1753 he made a treaty with them. They complained of their abuses at the hands of the private traders. Franklin was anxious to remove the causes for complaint. He wrote Governor Bowdoin of Boston for a copy of the [illegible] Massachusetts law [illegible] [illegible] method of [illegible].[1] Governor Bowdoin reviewed the act as

---

[1] Franklin's Works, Bigelow Ed. II [illegible]

operated in Massachusetts. He dwelt especially on the two effects of the trading house system": 1. By selling at wholesale rates they will not only be enabled to undermine the French trade but 2. will also remove the influence of the private trader.

Governor Dinwiddie, in 1757, referred to the passage of a similar trading house act in Virginia. The Assembly voted 5000 £'s. to commence the trade. Goods were sold at first cost. He urged the reasons already cited for the continuance of the act and

commended its use to all the colonies[11]. The trustees were directed to see the goods in lost on account of Indian hostilities. In 1765 however, the act of 1757 was revived and amended[12].

It is of interest also to note that South Carolina as early as 1716 used this method of trade[13]. Her commissioners formed a closer corporation than did those of any other colony. Their seal of corporate power was made the subject of trial before any court.

during and after the revolutionary times were agencies against English influences, as they had been of effect against the French dominion of that time.

We have noted Francis's interest in the system in 1800. Two years earlier than this in a letter concerning the training and increasing the friendship of the Indians" the alliance in knowledge

of the man[illegible]. He says: Private trading unless [illegible] should [illegible] have a good effect towards regulating the [illegible] trade of this [illegible] the inhabitants of the [illegible] traders, [illegible] such should [illegible] established [illegible] the [illegible]." In 1776 Congress accepted the report of the committee of which Franklin was a member[12] [illegible] to [illegible] in [illegible] the trade. The trade was to [illegible] control of [illegible] commissioners. Washington, during his administration, [illegible] this [illegible] made [illegible] through Franklin's influence, [illegible]

his annual addresses, he urges
upon Congress the necessity for
the safe establishment of such a
system. Says the 5th annual
address of Dec. 3, 1793,(1) "Next to a
rigorous execution of justice
on the violators of peace, the
establishment of commerce with
the Indian nations, in behalf of
the United States is most likely
to conciliate their attachment.
But it ought to be conducted without fraud, with constant and
plentiful supplies, with a ready
market for the commodities of
the Indians, and a stated price for
what they give in payment and
receive in exchange. Individuals
will not pursue such a traffic unless

ty is claimed by the [illegible] of
[illegible]
[illegible] United States [illegible]
[illegible]

[illegible] 1795 [illegible]
[illegible] not, [illegible] Washington's
suggestions, [illegible] (1) [illegible]
to remain in force the same.
The President of the United States
has to [illegible] the privilege of
[illegible] treating [illegible]
[illegible]
[illegible]
[illegible]
[illegible]
[illegible]

it were regarded its strength as a civilizing agent.(1) They aimed by it to accomplish two objects: one was the securing of the friendship of the Indians by supplying their wants, the other was the supplanting of the British trader in his influence over the Indians.

The reason given in the report of the Secretary of War in 1795 that the trading houses were established, as a [illegible] among the Southern [illegible] tribes as at the north and west [illegible] into friendly intercourse. One of these houses was located among the Creeks at Coleraine because of ease of access

(1) Annals of Congress I., 231ff., 283

both by and [illegible] by [illegible]. The [illegible] the means of [id]entifying the [illegible] of Chickasaw [illegible] of Indian [illegible], in [illegible] territory. The [illegible] the Indian [illegible] but [illegible] the [illegible] of the United States. [illegible]

Trade [illegible] regulated by the President, [illegible] to be introduced in order that the hunters might bring their [illegible]

[illegible]

[illegible] the trading

[illegible]

[illegible]

[illegible] carriage. Where licensed

traders procured these goods

from the Factors, they were

[illegible]

[illegible] rapid, [illegible]

[illegible]

[illegible] in [illegible]

[illegible]

[illegible]

[illegible]

[illegible]

adequate reward [illegible] the trade up to this time [illegible] may [illegible] advantage in the system, [illegible] obtained [illegible] to the [illegible] and [illegible] intentions [illegible] the traders; these good results [illegible] a sufficient [illegible] to [illegible]. It [illegible] time, using the same [illegible].

[illegible] the [illegible], [illegible] recommended, [illegible] of the chief agents for reducing the savages to civilization, that the trading houses [illegible] without [illegible],

in order that those things might be exchanged with a trade which would contribute more to their domestic welfare than the possession of "large but uncultivated fields". In his 3d. annual message he speaks of a system which would furnish necessaries in exchange for commodities at such moderate prices as would lead to no gain but even to some loss, as being a most conciliatory and useful effect upon the minds of Indians which would best secure their peace and good will." The message for '81 contains the same unquestioning approval of the plan. He says:

instead [illegible] aug-
mentation [illegible]
[illegible]
[illegible]
[illegible]
[illegible] in that [illegible]
[illegible]
[illegible]
[illegible]
[illegible]. The
message for 1807 refers in
a most [illegible] way to the
satisfaction manifested by
the Indians of the Missouri
and the Mississippi valleys, with
their [illegible]
[illegible]
[illegible] terms with the United
States.

The original [illegible] [illegible] [illegible] but [illegible] [illegible] the system. [illegible] the years [illegible] [illegible]. This [illegible] did not [illegible] community. The pictures had been established with the [illegible] sites: [illegible]; [illegible]; [illegible]; [illegible]; [illegible]; [illegible]; [illegible]; [illegible]; [illegible].

[illegible]

[illegible] many ad-vantages in this system seems sufficiently attested, [illegible]

[illegible]

[illegible] strain, [illegible] to [illegible]

[illegible]

The [illegible]

[illegible]

[illegible]

it has [illegible] established. 2, The [illegible]

[illegible] process, [illegible]

the [illegible] of the [illegible]

[illegible]

[illegible]

[illegible]

[illegible]

At the beginning of the [illegible]

[illegible], [illegible] the [illegible]

[illegible]

[illegible]

stronger through the succeeding

years up to the [illegible]

of the [illegible].

easily learn the peculiar manners and customs of the Indians and soon became an influential with the different nations with which he came in. Americans who were appointed to important positions here were, many of them, who were not acquainted with Indian methods nor did they know how to conciliate him in trade". The English gave all officers of the Indian Department military brevet rank and allowed them to bear titles of [illegible] in. This military rank obviated many difficulties by making uniform the various measures.

Gaudy clothes and beaded trappings and a little [illegible]

in the [illegible] of the natives. The [illegible] British [illegible] thought it not [illegible] the contents [illegible] the [illegible] with the Indians. They [illegible] themselves of the evil influences of designing interpreters. Trading houses were established by the United States officials in conjunction with military posts. The relative importance of the officials in each of these posts have not been clearly defined and much embarrassment arose from conflicting orders. The superintendents were too often uninterested in their duties and turned the official [illegible] over to less competent persons.

The English made many presents to the Indians. When they came to the understanding that the goods distributed throughout the factories were not to be given them, they lost confidence in a "Father" whom they thought so poor that he was unable to descend to the position of a small trader.

The United States Government attempted to use the same methods as those employed by the English. Either the amounts voted were insufficient or there was so great delay in transferring even these scanty means to the agents that they eventually lost control of the chiefs. A letter from the agent at

Ft. [illegible] reports to these insects as follows: "From the issue last day to twenty [illegible] [illegible], I am persuaded that no good can possibly result from this method but it promotes [illegible] much heart-burning and discontent. Those who receive their small allowance are scarcely satisfied either with the agent or the government and those who can receive nothing, being compelled to [illegible] are dissatisfied with both." The English government, on the other hand, is reported to have [illegible] [illegible], [illegible] [illegible] [illegible] of the [illegible] at the [illegible] [illegible] [illegible] among the Chippewas of [illegible]

Superior, Huron and Michigan and the Ottawas, Munsees and the Minnesagose.

The goods used in the trading houses were inferior to those of the traders. A Committee of investigation reported a large portion of the stock to consist of men's and women's [illegible] fine shoes, [illegible] hose, tea, Glauber's salts, [illegible], anti-[illegible] pills, [illegible], fancy [illegible], [illegible], without [illegible] cotton,

to purchase stores from the factors. Private traders were continually being issued from Tenn. The factors sold, as [illegible] to the English [illegible]. Credit was prohibited at the trading houses. As the Indian could not pay his debts until the close of the hunting season he was unable to obtain goods. The private trader accompanied the Indians to the hunting grounds where either might be most thoroughly [illegible] to. Abuses provision was made that there were to be no profits in the trade carried on by the government. Goods were sold at rates sufficient to pay for transport

in advance of the original cost.

Among the instructions sent out to the various Factors was one which forbade, urgently, the carrying on of any trade, commerce, or barter on the account of the Factors themselves. They were bound to the Government with satisfactory security, in the form of [illegible] bonds, that they would perform all their duties faithfully and return accurate accounts. Many Factors were supposed to have grown rich in the service.

[illegible]. Heavy [illegible] is
reported. [illegible]
showed [illegible]
[illegible].

Indian Slavery.

The Southern Indians were, in general, in a more advanced social stage than were the hunter tribes of the North. The tribes of Florida were an almost distinctively agricultural people. They raised enough maize and beans for subsistence during the greater portion of the year. It is thought that well authenticated traces of their palisaded villages and raised mounds are still visible. This accounts for the more ready conquest of these unwarlike tribes by the Spaniards. It may also explain the more ready inter-marriage of the Spanish

with the Indians and [illegible] the [illegible] of the natives to the policy of their [illegible].

The Spaniard came with his [illegible] notion that all things were made by [illegible] of the [illegible]. Natives [illegible] included in [illegible] notion of the "repartimiento system".[1] In the first, [illegible] the [illegible] of the Indians". Under the second form of the repartimientos, in 1497, feudal ideas become more notable. Land was granted "in the Indies", the grant including a certain number of natives to till the soil.[2]

1. Helps, Spanish Conquest I 52.
2. Helps Spanish Conquest I [illegible]

A few years later the "encomiendo" came into usage(1). By this form, the persons to whom Indians were assigned had the right to exact tribute from them. Payments were necessarily made, largely through labor.

In the meantime, Bobadilla, the successor of Columbus, seemed to have gone further and to have allowed the Spaniards to treat their Indians as laborers, to be taken to work anywhere, and without any restriction". The hardships of the natives under this last system need not be

We find no evidence of an [illegible] of Indian slavery among the English colonists. The Indian was, [illegible] the first [illegible] of the [illegible] system. The Negro formed the [illegible].

[illegible], [illegible] of the [illegible] in the [illegible] on the remaining [illegible] of [illegible]! By this unquestioned usage, [illegible] of [illegible] be [illegible] of the [illegible]

The duty of selling into slavery was enforced by a higher morality than that which had previously sacrificed the life of the victim.

But positive legislation on the subject comes again in Massachusetts. "None of the laws of this colony were printed until 1648."[1] As early as 1635, however, it was thought by the body of freemen that the magistrates had acquired too great power. With their knowledge in these, they succeeded to frame their celebrated declaration of rights known as "Body of Liberties". In the [illegible]

1. Palfrey. History of New England II 22

articles of which it is composed,
two of them have definite
reference to slaves. These
probably form the first
enactments establishing
slavery in America. One
article declares[1]: "There shall
never be any bond slaverie,
villinage or Captivitie amongst
us unless it be lawfull Captives
taken in just warres, and
such strangers as willingly
sell themselves or are sold
to us. ... This exempts none
from servitude who shall be
Judged thereto by Authoritie".

This may be regarded as
a restrictive clause. Here
and there slaves

(1) Mass. Hist. Soc'y. Coll. S. 3. VIII. 231.

institution of slavery was to continue, although confined to three classes of persons.

Slavery does not seem to have been sanctioned in the colony from a pecuniary standpoint. It was rather used as a measure of defence. By far the largest number of slaves belonged to the first of the three classes. [illegible] [illegible] to [illegible] namely those [illegible] of the [illegible]. The Indian was bound to acquiesce to a requirement [illegible] then that of his own [illegible]. The colonist must [illegible] [illegible] instruction

case all.

Man-stealing was made a criminal offense. It is argued from the act alone that children born in the colony were not enslaved. [illegible] this point however, there are wide differences of opinion.[1]

Dread and alarm of the colonists through the Pequot attacks caused them to take [illegible] in these [illegible] possibilities. Gov. Winthrop writing in 1637 of an attack and defeat of this tribe says: "The Prisoners were divided, some of those to the [illegible], and the rest to us, of these we send the male children to Bermuda [illegible]

1. See Moore, Hist. of Slavery in Mass. p. 28. Discussion [illegible]

women & maid children — are
disposed of [illegible] in ye towns".
A letter [illegible]
[illegible] the Pr[illegible]
[illegible] on the subject [illegible]
It suggests [illegible] method of
dealing with the Indian captives.
"I have with the [illegible]", he
writes [illegible], "[illegible]
to this [illegible], [illegible]
matter [illegible]
[illegible]
[illegible]
[illegible]
[illegible]
[illegible]
[illegible]
[illegible]
[illegible]

in exchange for bonds, which will be more [illegible] saleable for us than [illegible] [illegible], for I do not see how we can [illegible] until we get into stock [illegible] supplement to [illegible] business, for our children's children will surely see the [illegible] contingent business with respect, and that [illegible] [illegible] [illegible] freedom(?) [illegible] [illegible] secure, I must stay [illegible] [illegible] next pages. [illegible] emphasise [illegible] [illegible] [illegible] [illegible] [illegible] [illegible] cheaper [illegible] [illegible] [illegible] [illegible].

A similar [illegible] [illegible] [illegible]

To the criminality [illegible] by
the [illegible] of [illegible]
of Indians for the [illegible]
maintained by the [illegible]
In the [illegible] years of the
[illegible], it was
required that Indian [illegible]
[illegible]
because of the cost of maintaining
the delinquents [illegible]
might [illegible],
[illegible]
magistrates [illegible]
in the Indian [illegible]
[illegible]
[illegible]
[illegible]

slave law ever enacted in America was that passed by the United Colonies in [illegible].[1] It provided for the return to his master of any escaped servant. Such servant was to be given over to any person who claimed the services of the escaped party, providing he claimed the right of seizure through a magistrate's certificate. Upon the proof of the right of search, any magistrate was to grant

that is granted, and paying the charge thereof."

During this Period No 2, the number of instances was greatly enlarged. At a meeting of the Plymouth council in 1676 to consider the disposition of over one hundred captives, it was concluded, "upon serious and deliberate consideration and agitation concerning them, to sell the greater number into servitude".[1] It was further provided in 1676, that any who held Indian male captives were to dispose of them by the end of the year. Any who held their captives beyond the time stipulated were to forfeit them to the colony.[2]

colonies for 1675 includes the
sale of 188 captives, for which
397.13.[illegible] were received. The
account of an estate at Salem
in 1655 counts Indians among
the chattels. Besides the sheep,
silverware, napkins etc., there
was an "Indian maid and man
servant, they fulfilling their
respective indentures".(4)

It would appear that the
freedom of the natives was
attained at times through [illegible].
They were also freed on the
attainment of a certain age
after a term of service. The
Plymouth Court ordered the
release of a certain Indian woman
[illegible] her husband [illegible] the [illegible]

of our brothers of the "sum of three pounds silver money of New England" and have engaged to pay three pounds more in the same circle". The order further promises in the case of a 'Younge Indian', that he shall remain with his master until he reaches the age of twenty-four "and then to be released for ever".

"Conditional servitude, under indentures or covenants, had from the first existed in Virginia."[2] White servants, [illegible]

[illegible] in the [illegible] of [illegible]

[illegible]

[illegible]

[illegible]

of Indian [illegible] in

Virginia until the year 1657.

In this [illegible]

[illegible]

of Indian [illegible] and

[illegible] by the

English, [illegible]

[illegible]

[illegible] within ten days, five

hundred pounds of tobacco

[illegible]

by the [illegible]ing party.(1)

[illegible]

on the Indian [illegible]
[illegible]
setting, [illegible]
[illegible]
[illegible]
[illegible]
[illegible]
[illegible] of the country",
[illegible](1) [illegible]
[illegible]
[illegible]
[illegible] Indians, [illegible]
[illegible]
[illegible]
[illegible].

There is a [illegible]
[illegible]
[illegible]
[illegible]

for life, & those who came by land were slaves, they were to serve until they attained the age of thirty [illegible] were to be free. [illegible] imported was freed at the expiration of twelve years.[1] The term servant was made applicable later, contrary to the original intent, to Negroes. In consequence, the act was repealed in [illegible]82.

Therefore, all Indians sold as slaves were to be so regarded. This act would [illegible] those Indians [illegible] and other Indians. [illegible] provided that [illegible] in [illegible]

[illegible] remembered, [illegible]
might be traced with
[illegible] at [illegible] time.[2] [illegible]
with this [illegible] the [illegible]
based its [illegible] of [illegible]
[illegible] entire [illegible] [illegible]
brought into [illegible] in [illegible]
the year [illegible] [illegible],
any circumstances, it [illegible]
made [illegible] start". [illegible]

[illegible] [illegible], [illegible] [illegible] [illegible] [illegible] [illegible] [illegible] [illegible] [illegible] [illegible].

After the treaty of Albany in 1722 Virginia Indians were [illegible] to cross the Potomac river without license, and were not any of the Five Nations on the [illegible] [illegible] beyond the boundary line. If any [illegible] were to be punished by death or transportation.[1] Many of the [illegible] [illegible] [illegible] [illegible] regarding slavery in Virginia, contain the incapability to all persons of [illegible] [illegible] negroes, Indians or mulattoes. They cannot, in consequence, be [illegible] [illegible] for any [illegible] [illegible].[2]

ensued in New Sweden colony to any considerable extent, it is not even recognized as a part of the system. There are but few references to the Indian slavery apart from the Negro and mulattoes, the first direct instance occurred in 1644. A report to the West India Company says: "The captured Indians who might have been of considerable use to us as slaves, have been given to the soldiers as presents [illegible]

children who had been given into the hands of the English that they might be instructed".

As late as 174[illegible] Colonel Johnson wrote Governor Clinton of this usage as follows: "I am very glad your excellency has given orders to have the Indian children returned, who are kept by the Traders as pawns or pledges as they call it, but rather stolen from them, as the parents came at the appointed time to redeem them but they sent them away before hand, and as they were children of our Friends & allies and if they are not returned next spring it will convince what

1. N. Y. Col. Docs. V. 432.

the French took the violations i.e. that we [illegible] when the [illegible] slaves [illegible] [illegible]."(1)

Connecticut had some cases of Indian slavery. These were [illegible] used by the rules of the United Colonies. The General Court in 1650 ordered that all Indians who surrendered themselves within a stated time should not be sold "out of the country for slaves."(2) This [illegible] was granted them after ten years of faithful service. [illegible] of 1715 prohibiting the importation of [illegible](3) [illegible] were ineffective.

[illegible] allowance of the [illegible]ment of the Indian in the [illegible], their [illegible] [illegible], [illegible] [illegible], [illegible] in [illegible]; [illegible] [illegible] [illegible] their [illegible] [illegible], [illegible] [illegible] of the [illegible] of the colonists were counteractive of the good influence to be rendered by education and religion. These were of little effect so long as [illegible] were tolerated.

Biographical.

James Milton [illegible] was born at [illegible], in Grant County, Wisconsin, September 7th, [illegible]. He received his early training in a district school. By doing work outside of the regular course, he was prepared to enter the State Normal School at Platteville, Wisconsin. After completing the [illegible] course, he was graduated in [illegible].

He became assistant principal of the High School at [illegible], Wisconsin, for two years.

In September [illegible], he entered the Wisconsin State University as a [illegible] student. In [illegible], he

was elected to the junior class,
by a special vote of the faculty.
He was graduated in 1888,
giving the Valedictory Address.

He was elected Principal
of the High School at Burlington,
Wisconsin which position he
held two years.

In October 1890, he
entered the Johns Hopkins
University [illegible]. The
studies of history as a
major and political economy
and philosophy as subordinates,
He took extra courses in
administration and sociology.

He was elected a Fellow
in history in January 1892, and
[illegible] in June of the same year.

www.ingramcontent.com/pod-product-compliance
Lightning Source LLC
Chambersburg PA
CBHW060613030726
47498CB00005B/1656